tIS BOOK BELONGS
TO ...

D0279803

For Kersti Elliott

THE BIG BOOK OF OLD TOM

THE BIG BOOK OF
OLD TOM

Leigh HOBBS

ALLEN&UNWIN

SYDNEY • MELBOURNE • AUCKLAND • LONDON

Allen & Unwin
83 Alexander Street
Crows Nest NSW 2065
Australia
Phone: (61 2) 8425 0100
Email: info@allenandunwin.com
Web: www.allenandunwin.com

A Cataloguing-in-Publication entry is available
from the National Library of Australia
www.trove.nla.gov.au

ISBN 978 1 74331 844 7

Te

Set in 15 pt

This book wa

Marybor

dio
n St,

CONTENTS

OLD TOM

Angela Throgmorton lived alone and liked it that way. One day, while doing some light dusting, she heard a knock at the door.

There, on her front step, was a baby monster.

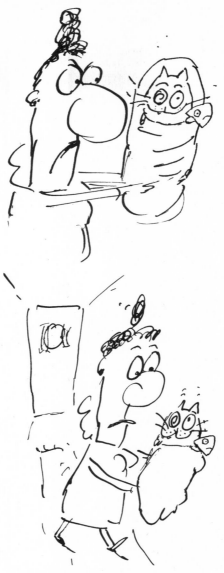

Angela was curious,
so she carried him in ...

and brought him up.

Angela had never fed a baby before,
and what a strange big baby he was!
She called him 'Old Tom'.

Old Tom grew up very quickly. In fact, it wasn't long before he outgrew his playpen.

And when he did, Angela gave him the spare room. It was all clean and neat.

Angela taught Old Tom how to behave.
'Sit up straight!' she would say.
'Elbows off the table.'

'Not too much on your fork.'
'Chew with your mouth closed.'

There was so much to learn.

But Old Tom loved bath time most of all,
when he could splash about and make a mess.

He always liked to look his best ...

especially when he went out to play.

At first, Angela ignored Old Tom's
childish pranks.

After all, she had things to do and dishes
to wash.

But her heart sank when *someone* forgot his manners.

Old Tom *tried* to be good ...

though sometimes he was a bit naughty.

'Aren't you a little too old for such things?'
Angela Throgmorton often asked.

As the months went by, Angela tried to keep
the house tidy.

It wasn't easy, as Old Tom seemed
to be everywhere.

There was no doubt about it,

he was a master of disguise.

Sometimes Angela heard strange noises
coming from the kitchen,

and whenever she had guests, Old Tom
would drop in unannounced.

Old Tom was out of control.

'When *will* you grow up?' Angela often
muttered under her breath.

Sometimes Old Tom went for a little walk
to the letterbox.

But Angela thought it best that he stay inside.
'You mustn't frighten the neighbours,'
she would say.

When babies came to visit ...

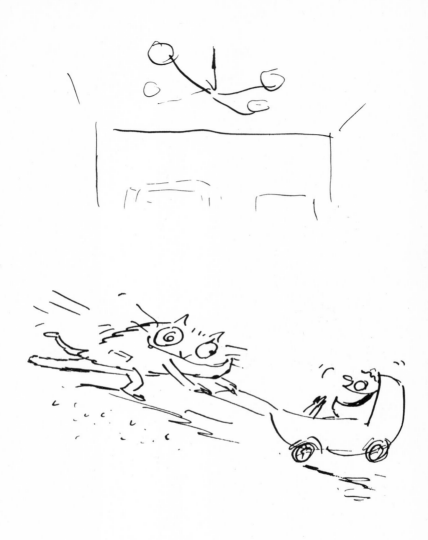

Old Tom loved to play.

'Heavens, what's that in the pram
with my baby!' cried one of Angela's friends
during afternoon tea one day.

It was Old Tom, of course.
Angela was extremely embarrassed.

By now, Angela was having trouble sleeping.

Her nerves were shattered,

and Old Tom's fur had given her
dreadful hayfever.

When she finally did
fall asleep, Old Tom was
often in her dreams.

Angela longed for the good old days,
when her home was in order ...

with everything in its place.

Whenever it was time to help with
the dishes, Old Tom felt sick.

He liked to sleep in, and enjoy a late breakfast on Angela's favourite armchair.

Angela was fed up.

Old Tom had to go.

'At last I have the house to myself!'
cried Angela Throgmorton.

It was a bold move,

but Angela thought it for the best.

Now she was free to scrub ...
and polish,
sweep and mop.

With Old Tom gone, her house would be spick and span once more.

By now Old Tom was in town,

where there were places to see
and people to meet.

PET
SHOP

In a pet shop nearby, he found new friends
to play with.

Some had feathers and one had fins.

But Fluffy the puppy was
Old Tom's favourite.

In the cinema next door the film had
just started.

When Old Tom wandered in ...

he was mistaken for a monster on the screen.

It was a wonderful surprise when
Old Tom found Happyland.

There were swings and slides,

places to hide,

children to play with ...

and an elephant to ride.

Old Tom was having a lovely time.

But not everyone was happy in Happyland.

When darkness fell, Old Tom was alone.

And when the storm came, he tried to be brave,

even when the thunder boomed.

For Old Tom there was
no breakfast or lunch,

or afternoon tea ...

while far away, Angela was alone in her clean
tidy home.

Old Tom tried and tried to find
someone to play with.

But he couldn't find one friendly face.

There was no fur on her floor, but Angela
still couldn't sleep.

And neither could Old Tom.

He had nowhere to go
and nothing to eat,

until at last he found food at the
bottom of a bin,

where he dreamt of his warm safe bed.

Angela was worried sick.

For poor Old Tom ...

the future looked bleak.

Suddenly there was a news flash:
'ORANGE FURRY MONSTER CAUGHT.'

'That monster is my baby!' cried Angela
Throgmorton.

In no time at all, she was off to the
pound to rescue Old Tom.

'Be quick!' Angela shrieked.

Inside his cage,
Old Tom had just begun to cry,

when suddenly he heard a big voice boom:
'I'm here for my baby!'

Angela was overjoyed.

And so was Old Tom.

OLD TOM

AT THE BEACH

Early one morning, Angela Throgmorton
and Old Tom left home.

They were off to the beach.

It had taken hours to pack.

Old Tom had never been to the beach before,

and he was eager to see the sights.

Angela soon made herself comfortable.

'Go and play,' she said.
'Don't wander too far,
and stay where I can see you.
Most importantly...

Angela went to sleep immediately
and Old Tom set off across the sand.

Nearby was a castle,

where he admired the view.

Old Tom decided to dig for treasure.

And, sure enough, he found lots straight away.

All this work made Old Tom hot,

so he ran to the ice-cream stand.

'What flavour do you want?'
asked the ice-cream man rudely.

Old Tom tried them all.

The ice-creams were good,
but the games looked better...

Old Tom joined in.

UP in the air,

DOWN on the ground,

and UP in the air again.

People were startled by Old Tom's strength.

The sand was getting hot
and the sun had gone to Old Tom's head.

Now was the time to test the water.

At first it felt a little strange,

but Old Tom soon floated like a leaf,
far out to sea.

He passed a friendly mermaid,

and bounced above a whale,

while Angela relaxed in the warm midday sun.

Suddenly...

Old Tom felt a nibble down below.

His pants had disappeared.

Adrift in an angry sea,

Old Tom was hooked by a flipper,

and hoisted high above the waves.

'What have we here?' asked Percy the Pirate.
Old Tom was afraid, but only a little bit.

The pirates soon made him feel welcome.
Percy the Pirate gave Old Tom a hat and a telescope.

It was Percy's birthday,

and the pirates were having a party.

They danced and they sang.

Pirates certainly knew how to have fun.

Though, during the party,

Percy the Pirate forgot his manners,

then caused a commotion

when he blew out the candles.

Later, Old Tom climbed the crow's nest,

and through his telescope spied Angela,
dozing in the sun.

Without warning the ship swayed.

Poor Old Tom fell into the sea.

He held his breath and sank beneath the waves.

Then he tickled a monster,

and saw a sea-beast wearing his pants.
They fitted perfectly.

When Old Tom ran out of air,

he was tossed about by a friendly octopus,

and delivered back to the beach.

It had been a big day for Old Tom,

and he needed a nap.

Angela looked at her clock.
It was time to go home.

Old Tom had lost all his things,

and *someone* was cross.

A few days later,

a mysterious box arrived.

When Old Tom unwrapped his parcel,

he found two flippers, one telescope
and his favourite pirate hat.

Then he taught Angela the Pirate Polka.

OLD TOM

GOES TO MARS

One day, Angela Throgmorton saw
a sweet little house for sale. 'I must
have it for my big baby,' she said.

'Do you deliver?' she asked.
'Of course, madam,' came the reply.
'Good, then I'll take it.'

Soon afterwards,
Old Tom's little house arrived.

'I've a surprise for you, Old Tom,' said Angela,
interrupting his late-afternoon nap.

'It's called a playhouse.
You can keep all your things in there.'

Old Tom loved surprises,
and this one was very special.

There were buttons and levers
and dials and switches.

So Old Tom pressed,

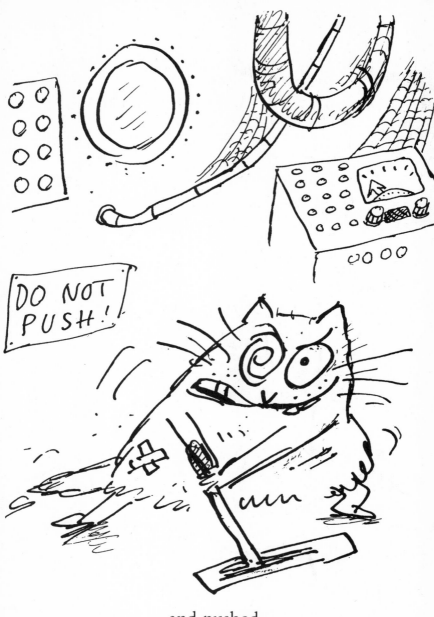

and pushed,

195

and turned,

and fiddled.

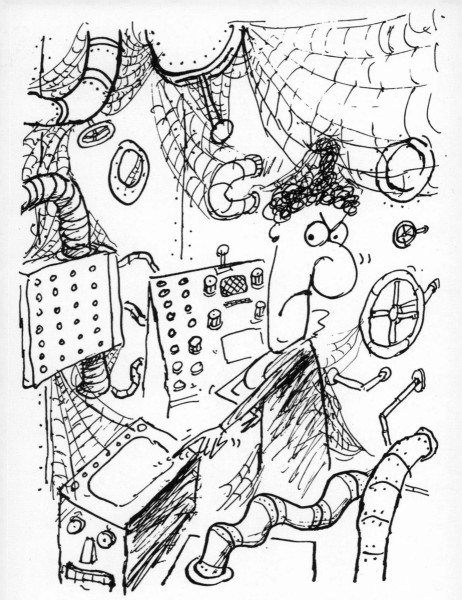

'This little house could do with a clean,'
said Angela Throgmorton.

So she dusted

and swept,

sponged, and scrubbed.

She was certainly fussy

when it came to her cleaning.

And it was while she was wiping

that Angela discovered Old Tom had a secret.

He had found a map, and was going to Mars.

HOW TO GET TO MARS

Angela tried to change Old Tom's plans.

She thought a nice story might distract him.
But his mind was made up.

Old Tom was off to outer space.

So Angela decided to help.
She made pretty curtains,

and sewed a special
cushion for his trip.

She even made smart striped awnings
in case Old Tom flew too close to the sun.

'What an improvement,'
said Angela, 'even if I do say so myself.'

Angela baked a cake
for Old Tom's journey,

and his favourite biscuits too.

Helping in the kitchen made Old Tom tired.

So he relaxed a little,
and thought about his trip.

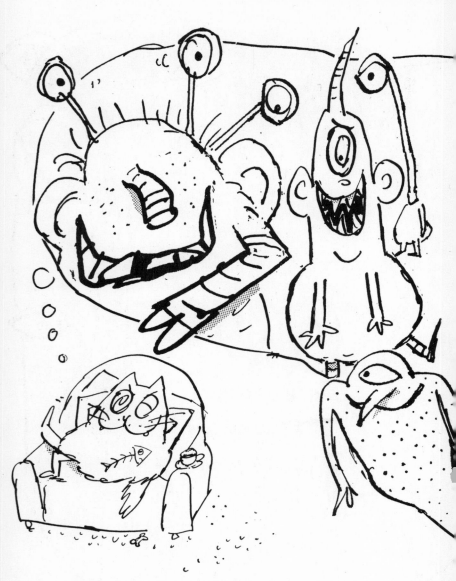

He couldn't wait to meet a Martian,
and make new Martian friends.

And if they made him King of Mars . . .

he could eat and drink . . .

everything
that he wanted.

Just then a Martian spoke,
and Old Tom woke up.

'I wouldn't mind some help
around the house!' it said.

So while Angela
cleaned up *someone's* mess,

Old Tom assembled his essential
Mars survival kit.

Angela had made Old Tom
a splendid space suit.

'You can wear this on Mars.
Try it on now!'

'And here's a lovely helmet
to go with it!'

'You look wonderful!' said Angela,
as she wiped away a little tear.

In the evening, Old Tom
did some last-minute packing,

and then got ready for bed.

'You'll need a good night's sleep if you're off to Mars tomorrow,' snapped Angela Throgmorton.

For once,
Old Tom did what he was told.

But Angela tossed and turned all night.

After breakfast, she reminded
Old Tom to be careful,

then farewelled her brave little spaceman.

It was time for him to go.

'Don't forget your lunch!'
said Angela Throgmorton.

She was already missing him terribly,

when suddenly Angela spied a
spot she hadn't scrubbed.

So she scampered up a ladder . . .

as Old Tom prepared for blast off.

At last the time had come!

He turned his dials
and pressed his buttons.

With a bang and a roar
and a flash,
Old Tom left earth,

bound for Mars at last.

Old Tom's essential Mars
survival kit rolled about

as he activated the extra thruster to escape earth's gravity.

As Old Tom shot
through the sky,

old tom

he peered out for one last look,

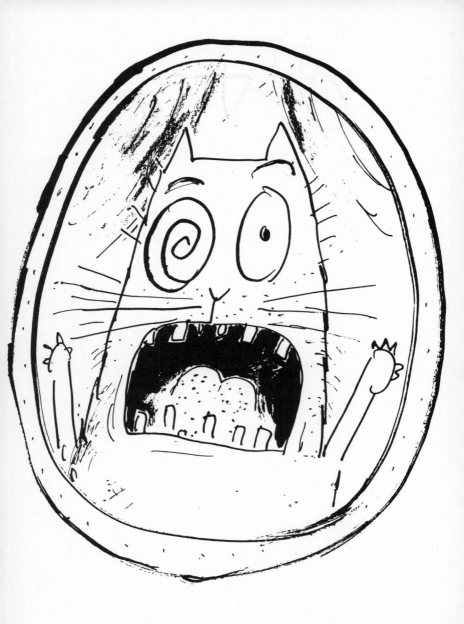

and saw something frightful.

Old Tom was not alone.

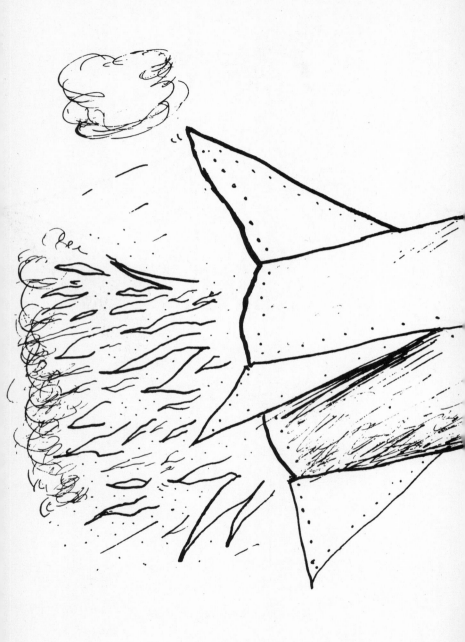

Angela Throgmorton
was Mars-bound too.

The view was spectacular.

But, inside, the danger light was flashing.

Old Tom was off course . . .
and overloaded.

Angela was angry.

She had work to do at home,

and now she was off . . .

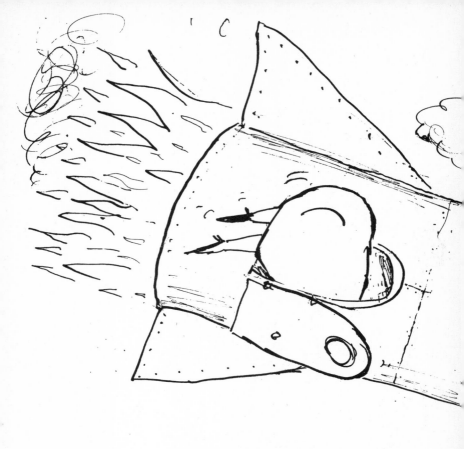

to outer space.

Old Tom wrestled with the controls.

Angela was no help at all.

They hurtled towards Mars

as Angela served afternoon tea.

'We're here!' she shrieked.
Angela was excited too.

Old Tom prepared for landing.
He wanted to make a good impression.

He put on the brakes,

and disengaged the thruster.

His arrival caused a sensation.

Old Tom wanted to make new friends,

but the Martians wouldn't play.

'This doesn't look like Mars to me!'
cried Angela Throgmorton.

It had been a long, long trip . . .

and Angela was a wreck.

Old Tom's adventure was over.

Angela's too.

She was glad to be home.

'There'll be no more trips to Mars
for us,' said Angela Throgmorton.

While she settled back into
life on earth,

Old Tom stayed in his room and sulked.
Only one thing could cheer him up.

And it arrived early the next morning.

Old Tom had promised to be good.

'Let's hope it lasts!'
said Angela Throgmorton.

OLD TOM'S
GUIDE TO BEING GOOD

'I'm tired of the same old faces at my garden parties,' said the Queen with a sigh.

'Why not pick a name from the telephone book, Your Majesty?' suggested Sir Tassel Windburn, her able secretary.

'Splendid,' said the Queen.
Soon the royal finger stopped at a surname
beginning with 'T'.

And so, when Old Tom went to collect the
mail one day,

there was a fancy-looking letter, for Angela
Throgmorton.

She was enjoying a well-earned rest, having
cleaned the house from top to bottom.

But this was a letter that couldn't wait.
A royal invitation for two, for afternoon tea.

Angela knew the Queen was fussy about good manners. So she dressed up and wrote back straight away.

Angela had done her best to bring Old Tom up nicely.

He often happily helped around the house,

and sometimes did two chores at once.

But now that he was to meet the Queen,

Old Tom needed extra instruction in
how to be good.

Lavinia, darling...
lovely to see you.

Angela invited a friend for tea.
'Pretend it's the Queen and practise your
manners,' she said.

Old Tom had learnt from his lessons that a
nice smile is always handy.

He was eager to please and keen to be good.

That thing... It looked at me.

So, when Angela's guest felt a little unwell, kind Old Tom kept an eye on her.

Meanwhile, Angela went on with her eating instructions. 'If offered cake,' she said, 'say yes please, and thank you, and don't drop your crumbs.'

There was a lot to remember, but Old Tom
was pleased with his progress.

Though Angela felt there was still work to be done.

In fact, Angela was desperate.

But time had run out and Old Tom was as
good as he was going to get.

So Angela and Old Tom packed their bags
and off they went.

Angela was excited . . .

and so was Old Tom.

After his journey, Old Tom was tired.

PASSPORTS

'I've never seen anything like this before,'
said the passport man.

At the hotel,

Angela explained that she was on a royal visit.

Then, in the evening, Old Tom and Angela
practised their curtsies and bows.

Angela put on some gloves and pretended
to be the Queen.

'Kiss my hand,' she said.

In the morning, Angela got up bright and
early. Old Tom had to have a bath …

and she was needed to remove difficult
oily patches.

This was a big day, and Old Tom planned
to look especially beautiful.

So, all morning, he combed and brushed and fussed and even had his nails done.

When the arrival of lunch stopped him
cleaning his teeth,

he still remembered his manners, and gave
a big smile.

Luckily, Old Tom's good looks hadn't gone to his head.

Angela, too, had spent hours getting ready.
Now it was time for afternoon tea.

So Old Tom and Angela caught a bus to
the palace.

When they arrived, Angela whispered,
'Now, remember your lessons and you'll
blend in quite nicely.'

Angela had expected only three for tea.
But she was polite and hid her disappointment.

Old Tom was on his best behaviour,

while Angela began to introduce herself
and make polite conversation.

'Angela Throgmorton's my name,' she said,
'and I'm here to meet the Queen.'

'Aren't we all?' replied Sir Cecil Snootypants.

At first, Old Tom was a little shy.

But soon he relaxed and made himself
comfortable.

Angela kept an eye on things and whispered
helpful hints when no one was looking.

Old Tom remembered to look people
straight in the eye and make them feel special.

Then he had a rest from being good and
made himself a sandwich.

Being good had certainly improved
his appetite.

Old Tom made friends quickly and even found a favourite.

He was careful, of course, to leave room
for dessert.

Meanwhile, Angela was having a lovely time.

'What an unusual hat!' mumbled Boswell
Croswell.

'I'm glad you like it,' was her gracious reply.

The afternoon-tea party was now in
full swing.

'I hear the Queen has been delayed,'
said Lady Arabella Volcano to her
husband Horace.

While chatting to Sir Basil Bossy and his charming wife Babette, Angela noticed that Old Tom had gone.

She excused herself and began to search.
Angela tried to tempt Old Tom out with a
fresh chicken leg.

Angela described Old Tom to everyone
she met.

'Oh, my goodness!' cried Sir Bertie Boodle.

'Good gracious!' shrieked Lady Winifred
Pineapple De Groote and her husband
Sir Ernest.

He has one eye, pointy ears and a hairy face.

'It can't be human!' cried Clarissa Cul-de-Sac just before she fainted.

Angela had mislaid
Old Tom, and wanted
him back before the
royal host arrived.

'By the way, where *is* the Queen?' asked Sir
Dalvin Dooper.

Suddenly there was silence, apart from a
tiny shriek from Lady Pineapple.

Her Majesty had arrived at last ...

and she had company.

Angela was thrilled to see Old Tom and
nearly forgot her manners.

But not for long, of course.

'So you are my *other* special guest! I've
already met Old Tom,' said the Queen.
'And what jolly fun we've had!'

Her Majesty insisted that they stay the night.

After dinner there was a royal tour.
'That's my throne,' said the Queen.
And then it was time for bed.

The comfort of her guests was most
important. So that ...

More toast and some marmalade too... please.

Certainly ma'am.

... at breakfast, even if the Queen *had* seen Old Tom's little mistake, she was too polite to comment.

Goodbye!

Soon it was time to say goodbye.
The Queen had her royal duties and
Angela had work to do around the house.

As for Old Tom, he was happy with a kiss
from Angela, his guide to being good.

A FRIEND FOR
OLD TOM

Life wasn't always this good for Old Tom.

These days he has a cosy warm bed on cold nights.

And a cool swimming pool on hot days.

Whenever Old Tom is out late,
someone stays awake and worries about him.

And if he sleeps in or feels a little unwell,
someone brings him breakfast in bed.

Of an evening, Old Tom likes to relax . . .

before dinner is served by someone who loves him.

Even if he forgets his manners,
Old Tom knows that all will be forgiven

and that someone will clean up after him.

Angela Throgmorton likes her house neat.
Which is why a visit to Old Tom's room
often comes as a horrible . . .

surprise!

Life would be easier for Angela if she
had a little help around the house.

But her little helper never seems to be
around when she needs him.

Of course, Angela is used to this by now.
She knows that when the work is nearly done,
Old Tom may well turn up . . .

somewhere unexpected.

Angela has always tried her best to be strict.
But she found out very early on

just how hard it was to stay cross with Old Tom.

There was a time long ago when Old Tom
had no name or place to call home,

and no warm, cosy bed on cold nights.

He was too hot in summer

and too cold in winter.

He gasped in autumn

and sneezed and wheezed through spring.

He had no one at all to protect him.

There was no relaxing before dinner.

In fact, there was often no dinner at all.

Maybe just a nibble now and then.

But that was never enough.

What he needed most were warm and
gentle arms around him.

He did his best to put on a happy face.

But that never seemed to help.

He was all alone.

Not far away lived a woman called
Angela Throgmorton.

Angela was always busy.
There was much to do around the house.

She had a spare room. It was all spick and span.

At the end of each day,
when her housework
was done,

Angela cooked a meal . . .

just for one.

Once a week Angela Throgmorton met her
friend Lavinia for afternoon tea.

On this particular day just as she left home,

someone found a *very* pleasant place to take a nap.

Angela didn't stop to find out
why a crowd had gathered.

She had other things on her mind.

She knew, as usual, Lavinia would have lots
to report about her *wonderfully busy* family life.

'Lucky you,' said Lavinia. 'Living alone must be divine. No one to care for. No one to clean up after . . .'

One hour later, Lavinia was still talking.
'And of course, no one to have to cook for.'
Angela did her best to put on a happy face.

But it didn't help.
Because she knew that tonight . . .

like every other night,

414

it would be . . .

dinner for one. Again.

But at least *she* had dinner.

Outside, someone knew what he was looking for.

While inside, Angela knew what she was missing.

Someone had a feeling he knew
where he belonged.

Now all he had to do was get there.

Later that night there was a tap! tap! tap!
on Angela's window. But she didn't hear it.

Later still, there was a knock! knock! knock!
on Angela's front door . . .

but she didn't hear that either.

So someone made himself as comfortable as he could and settled down for the night.

In the morning, Angela had the strangest feeling
that she wasn't alone. However, there was work
to be done so she thought little of it.

There were dishes to do,

teapots to polish,

a garden gnome to
look after . . .

and of course the spare room *always* had
to have its daily dust.

Today Angela was grateful for her household chores.

With so much to keep her busy,
her troubles were soon forgotten.

In fact, she almost began to cheer up.

Then, while doing some light dusting,
Angela heard a knock at the front door.

There on her doorstep was a baby monster.

Angela carried him in. She named him 'Old Tom'.

That was a long time ago, and now Old Tom has almost grown up.

But living with Old Tom hasn't always been easy for Angela Throgmorton . . .

or for the neighbours either.

Early on, Angela thought school might help
Old Tom learn to fit in.

He certainly made an impression.

But it wasn't the right one.

STRANGE
BEHAVIOUR
in the
WILD

And so Old Tom's first day at school
was also his last.

Things hadn't turned out quite as Angela had hoped. She would have to bring up Old Tom all on her own.

Back at home they had a heart-to-heart chat.
Old Tom seemed keen to be good.

In fact, he appeared eager to improve in all ways.

So they had tea and cake to celebrate.

Though they may have begun celebrations
a little too early.

Sure enough, every now and then Old Tom

needed a gentle reminder about how to be good.

And Angela often had to stand guard outside
his bedroom to make sure he cleaned up.

It seemed Angela's work was never quite done.

These days, though, it's not *all* work for
Angela Throgmorton.

She still meets Lavinia for afternoon tea.
But now *someone* has her own busy life to chat
about. What's more, she can't stay for long.

Angela Throgmorton is eager to get home.

After all, there's a meal to prepare,
and it's dinner for two . . .

followed by a little bedtime story.

Every night, just before he falls asleep, a
certain someone thinks how lucky he is . . .

and so does Angela Throgmorton.

A word from the author

I don't particularly dislike cats; it's just that I am allergic to them. In any case, I am most definitely a dog person. And Old Tom is more like an Australian cattle dog, or blue heeler, perhaps with a touch of Tasmanian devil, than he is a cat. Well, in my mind, anyhow.

In November 1992, I kissed a large envelope goodbye as I dropped it into a post box. The envelope was addressed to the senior editor at Penguin Children's Books, and it contained a short letter introducing myself and a furry, orange one-eyed feline monster called Old Tom.

Already rejected by a number of publishing houses, I was beginning to feel like Old Tom. And so I had decided that this was going to be my last attempt. In fact, somewhere I recall writing in large letters: 'Posted letter today. Forget it.'

Within a week, I had received a reply from the senior editor I'd written to, who said that she loved Old Tom and thought we should meet.

I was thrilled. Old Tom, it seemed, had found a home at last!

Leigh Hobbs

A note from the editor

In 1992 I was a senior editor at Penguin Books in the children's publishing department. One day a large envelope arrived. In it was a picture book dummy, with the words 'OLD TOM' on the cover accompanied by a loose, dynamic and hilarious illustration of a large, dishevelled cat holding the skeleton of a fish.

It was love at first sight! I was captivated by the expressiveness of Leigh Hobbs' character – in just a few pen-and-ink lines he had conveyed the most complex emotions. As I turned the pages, I experienced a telltale shiver up my spine, which meant that I was looking at the real thing: that Old Tom had to be published.

I adored Old Tom's relationship with Angela. It reminded me of my own relationship with my then seven-year-old son. For me, the stories of Old Tom and Angela have always been about a mother and a son and how they inhabit different worlds, can drive each other mad, yet share an unbreakable bond and will defend each other to the end.

My thanks go to my wonderful mentor, Julie Watts, the publisher at Penguin at the time, who gave

Leigh and me the freedom to develop that first Old Tom book, saying to us, 'Now go into that room and make a book together.'

Over twenty years later, Old Tom is a favourite with my grandchildren, has eight books to his name, and stars in a successful TV series too. Nothing is more satisfying than seeing the enduring appeal of the first of Leigh's brilliant creations.

ERICA WAGNER

A little bit about the author

Artist and author Leigh Hobbs works across a wide range of artistic mediums, but is best known for the children's books he writes and illustrates. These feature his characters Old Tom, Horrible Harriet, Fiona the Pig, the Freaks in 4F, Mr Badger and, of course, Mr Chicken.

Leigh's book *Mr Chicken Goes to Paris* was shortlisted for the Prime Minister's Literary Awards and is a very popular seller at the Louvre Museum Bookshop in Paris. It was also shortlisted for the Children's Book Council of Australia Book of the Year Awards, as was *Horrible Harriet* and *Old Tom's Holiday*.

Leigh is often asked if any of his characters are based on him. He admits that there may well be a little of himself in each of them.

You can read more about Leigh at
www.leighhobbs.com

Also by Leigh Hobbs
and available from
Allen & Unwin...

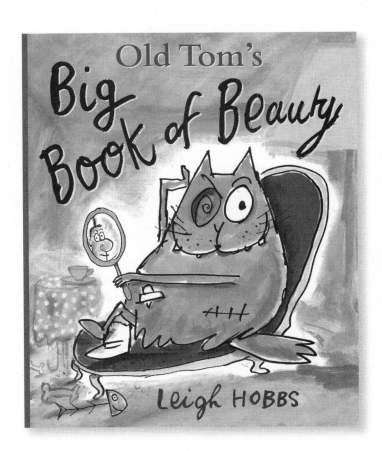

Old Tom's Big Book of Beauty

LEIGH HOBBS

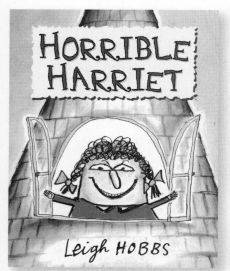

HORRIBLE HARRIET

Leigh HOBBS

HOORAY FOR
HORRIBLE
HARRIET

Leigh HOBBS

Horrible Harriet's
INHERITANCE

IN HER
OWN
WORDS

HH

ASSISTED BY

Leigh HOBBS

Mr Chicken goes to Paris

Leigh HOBBS

Mr Chicken lands on LONDON

Leigh HOBBS

Leigh HOBBS

Mr Badger
and the
Big Surprise

Leigh HOBBS

Mr Badger
and the
Missing Ape

Leigh HOBBS

Mr Badger
and the
Difficult Duchess

Leigh HOBBS

Mr Badger
and the
Magic Mirror